Butter Teeth

PAGE PUBLISHING, INC.
New York, NY

First originally published by Page Publishing, Inc. 2018

ISBN 978-1-64082-441-6 (Paperback)
ISBN 978-1-64082-442-3 (Digital)

Printed in the United States of America

Butter Teeth

Jada Cooper

Brush those chompers, scrub them good before mouth bugs build a neighborhood. They'll build houses left and right, eat your teeth both day and night.

Some open businesses and build schools, barbershops and swimming pools. Sometimes they build big hotels that make your mouth have nasty smells. They'll use your tongue as a diving board, make your teeth green as a gourd.

4

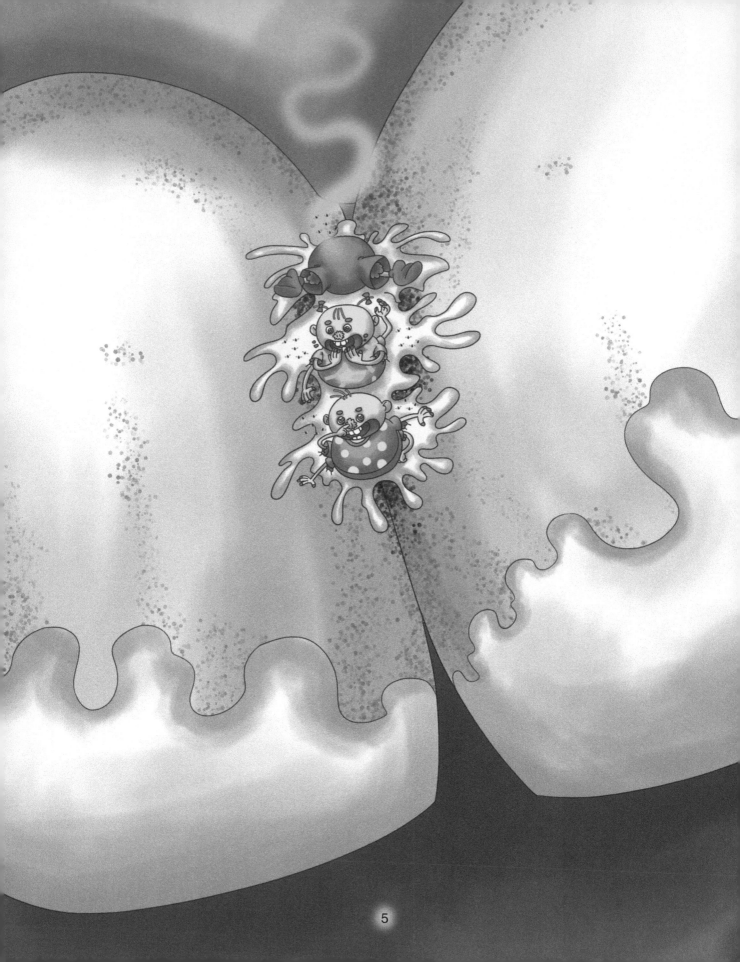

Sometimes they play hide-and-seek and get stuck between your teeth. They'll use your gums like busy streets if you don't brush away sweet treats. They fill your mouth with icky clutter, make your teeth yellow like butter.

All are green with purple hair, weird orange eyes that like to stare. They're always rude, never say please; make your breath smell like Swiss cheese. They never wipe their stinky feet, leave freckle footprints on your teeth. Some of them ride blue giraffes who eat old food and don't take baths.

None of them ever brush their hair
or change their socks and underwear.

Brown toenails that smell like burps, their favorite food is always dessert. Stinky underarms with lots of hair! You can't see them but they're there.

They all have pets that look like rats
who wear big shoes and matching hats.

They never pick up any trash, like to smell their nasty stash.

Some ride elephants; those are the worst! They stomp holes in teeth and make them hurt. Then the slimy goo goes in, and all the mouth bugs jump right in.

It's a party in your mouth, brush those teeth and kick them out! There's not one mouth bug who can stand the sight of floss in your hand!

All of them fear the mouthwash tide, leaves them nowhere else to hide. They'll get rinsed right down the sink with all their pets and nasty stink!

Get rid of their whole neighborhood, brush those chompers and scrub them good!

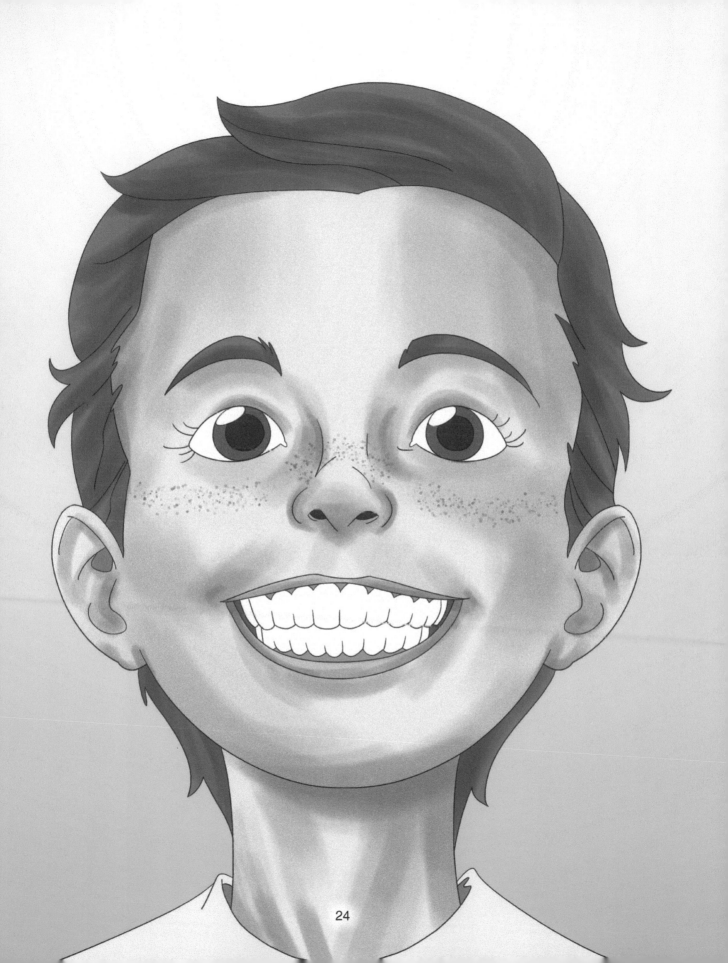

About the Author

Jada Cooper is an author who lives in Alabama with her husband, Jeremiah, and her two sons, Brody and Maddox. Her passion is using humor and creativity to inspire kids to have healthier habits.

CPSIA information can be obtained
at www.ICGtesting.com
Printed in the USA
BVHW021051180322
631854BV00018B/49

9 781640 824416